Disney's

THE RESCUERS DOWN UNDER

Far away, in the wild and rugged land of the
Australian outback, there lived a little boy named
Cody. Cody spent his days exploring the rocky
cliffs and crevices around his home. But, more
than anything, Cody loved to play with his

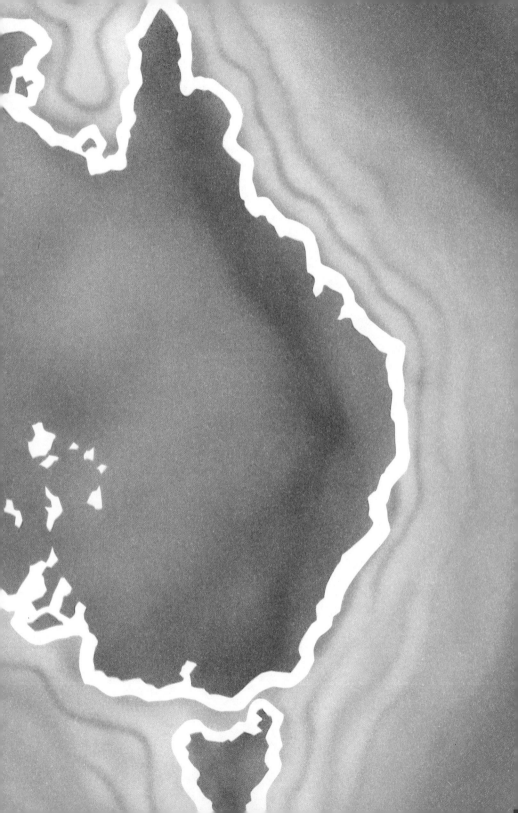

First American Edition. Copyright © 1993
The Walt Disney Company. All rights
reserved under international copyright
conventions. Published in the United States
by Grolier Enterprises Inc., Danbury,
Connecticut. Originally published in
Denmark as Bernard og Bianca S.O.S. fra
Australien by Gutenberghus Gruppen,
Copenhagen, in 1991. ISBN: 0-7172-8321-6

Manufactured in the United States.

C D   3 4 5 6

animal friends. He had even learned to talk to them and to understand their language.

One day, when Cody was out hiking, he met his friend Faloo, the kangaroo. She looked very worried.

"Cody!" cried Faloo, breathlessly. "You must come at once. Marahute, the great golden eagle, is trapped in a poacher's net high up on a cliff. You're the only one who can free her!"

"I'll get her loose!" Cody declared. "Let's go."

Cody quickly climbed on Faloo's back and hung
on tightly as she took off. Faloo and Cody raced
over the outback until they reached the bottom of
a steep cliff.

"Be careful," Faloo called, as Cody began the
dangerous climb to the top.

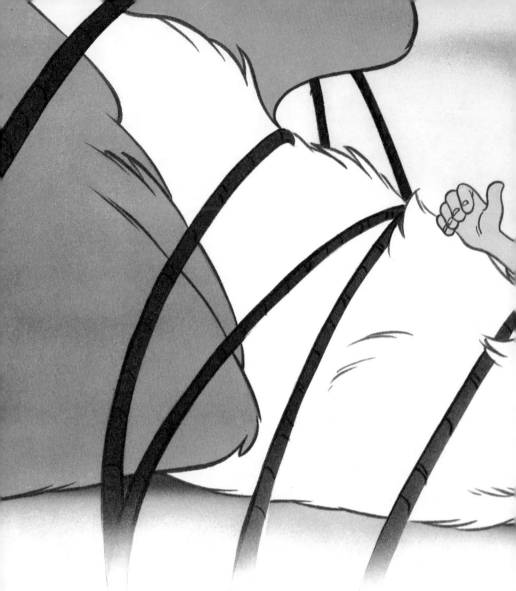

When Cody reached the top of the cliff, he
found Marahute trapped in a poacher's net. She
was screeching and struggling to free herself.

After Cody cut the thick ropes, Marahute
spread her wings. As she stretched, one of her
wings accidentally hit Cody. He tumbled off
the edge of the cliff!

"Help!" shouted Cody, as he plunged toward the sharp rocks below.

The great bird swooped down through the air until she was directly beneath the boy. Cody landed on her feathery back with a thud!

Cody clung to Marahute's neck as she took him for the ride of his life! They flew over steep cliffs and through winding gorges until they reached her nest. Marahute checked her eggs to make sure they were unharmed.

Then she gave Cody one of her precious feathers, to thank him for freeing her from the poacher's clutches.

On his way home, Cody discovered a little
mouse who had also been caught in a poacher's
trap. The poor thing was dangling helplessly
from a rope. But when Cody bent down to free it,
the mouse shouted, "No! It's a trap! Be careful!"

The warning was too late. The grass and
branches beneath the mousetrap hid a deep,
dark hole. When Cody freed the mouse, the
branches gave way and he fell into the pit!

"Now I've got you!" thundered a voice from
above. Cody looked up to see the face of the
poacher, Percival McLeach. A grinning lizard
was by his side.

McLeach yanked Cody out of the hole. "Well, Joanna," he said to the lizard. "It looks like we caught us a boy — a boy with a golden eagle feather!"

Then McLeach shoved Cody into the cage on his truck. "You're staying there until you tell me where I can find that eagle," he told Cody with a sneer. "That bird is worth millions to me, boy — dead or alive!"

Luckily, the little mouse had been watching, and he raced off to the animal telegraph office to send for help.

Meanwhile, on the other side of the world, two mice were dining in a fancy restaurant. Bernard was about to ask his friend, Miss Bianca, to marry him.

"Miss Bianca, will you . . ." Bernard began, but he dropped the ring! "Uh . . . excuse me," he said. Then he dived under the table to look for it.

By the time he found it, Bianca was reading a message. "Oh dear! We are needed back at headquarters," she exclaimed.

Without further delay, the two mice raced back to The Rescue Aid Society headquarters. There they learned that they were to go on a mission. A boy named Cody had been kidnapped, and Bernard and Bianca were chosen to help him.

Bernard and Bianca asked Wilbur the albatross to fly them to Australia.

"Sure," Wilbur told them as he looked out the window at the falling snow. "When do you want to go . . . the middle of June?"

"Tonight," said Bianca, and she explained their mission. Wilbur agreed to help them.

Soon Bernard and Bianca were on their way.
Bianca shouted out directions as Bernard held on
for dear life.

"Let's take a train next time!" sputtered
Bernard. He was greatly relieved when he finally
saw the sunny shores of Australia. But the
scary ride was not over yet.

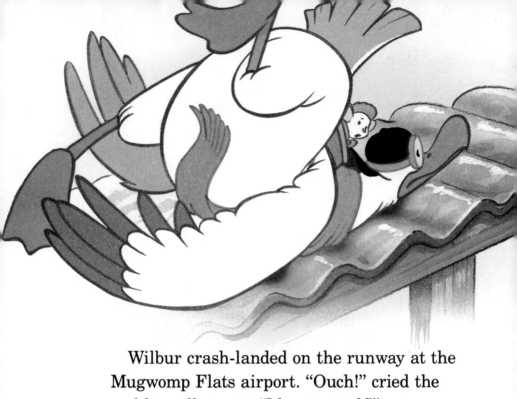

Wilbur crash-landed on the runway at the Mugwomp Flats airport. "Ouch!" cried the reckless albatross, "I hurt myself!"

"You'll have to be more careful next time, mate," said Jake, the Australian mouse who worked at the airport. Bernard had to agree.

Since Wilbur was hurt, Jake agreed to help
Bernard and Bianca cross the outback.

"There's nothing like a ride on the back of a
flying squirrel," said Jake with a chuckle.

Bernard soon found out what Jake meant. It
was a wild ride! Flying with Wilbur had been
easy compared to this!

As Bernard and Bianca were on their way, Cody was getting to know some of McLeach's other captives. There was a sad kangaroo named Red; a frustrated koala bear named Krebbs; and Frank, a frill-necked lizard, who was trying to get out of his cage.

Amazingly, Frank was able to pick
the lock with
his tail!

But in order to free his friends,
the small lizard still had to reach
a set of keys hanging on a hook
high up on a wall. He stood on a
box and reached for them.

Suddenly, Joanna barged in and chased poor
Frank back into his cage.

Meanwhile, Bernard, Bianca, and Jake were
getting closer. Luckily, the little mouse who
had sent the telegram to the Rescue Aid Society
had told them just where to find Cody.

Finally, the mice arrived at McLeach's compound.
But they were surprised at what they saw.
McLeach was letting Cody go!

"I don't need you anymore," he told Cody. "Your
bird's dead. Someone shot her right out of the sky."

Then McLeach smiled an evil smile.
"Too bad about those eggs. They'll never hatch
without their mother. They'll get cold and die with
no one to take care of them!"

Oh, no! thought Cody, *I've got to save poor
Marahute's eggs!* He quickly set off for the nest.

Marahute wasn't really dead. The clever
McLeach was just trying to trick Cody into
leading him to the nest of the great eagle.
As McLeach followed Cody in his truck, the
mice sneaked aboard, hoping to warn the boy.

When the truck reached the cliff, the three
mice hopped off to warn Cody. They found him at
Marahute's nest.

"It's a trap!" shouted Bianca. "McLeach is trying to capture the eagle. We must warn her!"

But it was too late! Marahute had already come back, and as she swooped down to her nest, McLeach threw a net right over her!

Marahute's angry cries rang out as McLeach
used a crane to pull her up.

"Oh, no!" shouted Cody. "This is all my fault!
I've got to help her!" Before the mice could
stop him, Cody leaped into the air and grabbed
hold of the net that held the golden eagle.

McLeach dropped the net into the cage on his truck. "Well, well, Joanna," he laughed. "It looks like we've caught two foolish birds with one net!" Bianca and Jake hurried to help Cody and Marahute, while Bernard stayed behind to watch the eggs.

The wicked poacher wasn't finished yet. Lowering the lizard toward Marahute's nest, he said, "Eat those eggs, Joanna. We want this eagle to be the last of her kind. Then she'll be even more valuable when we sell her to a zoo!"

Bernard quickly hid Marahute's eggs in a crevice. Then he rolled some rocks back into the nest — rocks that looked exactly like eggs!

Joanna didn't see Bernard when she reached the nest. With a big smile, the greedy lizard bit into one of the "eggs" and cracked a tooth! So, instead of eating them, she pushed the "eggs" over the edge of the cliff and left.

Back at Mugwomp Flats, Wilbur had recovered from his injury. He was on his way to find Bernard and Bianca.

Wilbur finally found Marahute's nest.

"Wonderful!" said Bernard with a smile. As he rolled the eggs back into the nest he said, "You're just in time, Wilbur! Sit on these." Wilbur did as he was told, but he wasn't too happy about it.

Then Bernard quickly climbed up to help his friends, but McLeach's truck was gone!

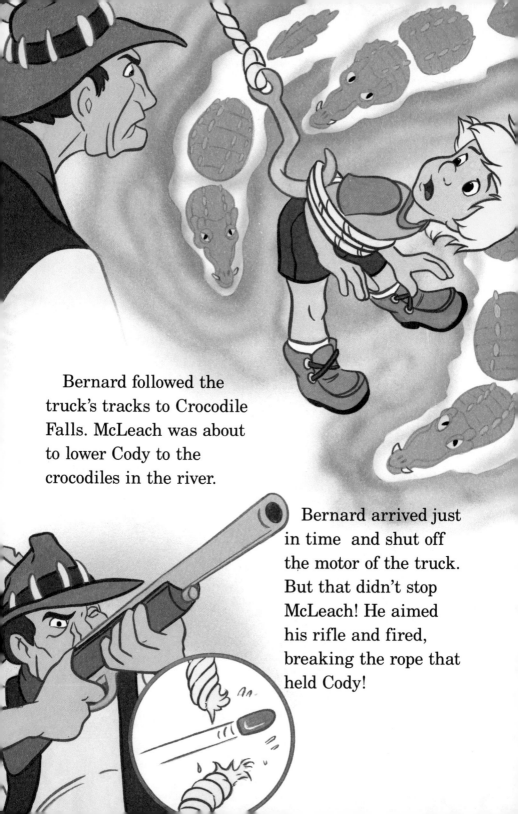

Bernard followed the truck's tracks to Crocodile Falls. McLeach was about to lower Cody to the crocodiles in the river.

Bernard arrived just in time and shut off the motor of the truck. But that didn't stop McLeach! He aimed his rifle and fired, breaking the rope that held Cody!

Cody fell into the water with a splash.

Bernard rushed to help him. "I hope I know what I'm doing," he muttered. With Joanna snapping at his heels, the brave little mouse ran between McLeach's legs. With a giant thud, Joanna crashed into her master, knocking all three of them into the water.

Bernard grabbed hold of the rope that still
bound the little boy. Not only did he have to save
Cody from the crocodiles, but also from a dangerous
waterfall! If they were swept over the edge, they
would surely be drowned.

Just when all hope seemed lost, they heard the sound of beating wings! It was Marahute! Bianca and Jake had managed to free the great bird from the cage, and she had come to rescue Bernard and Cody!

Marahute lifted them out of the water just in time. McLeach was not so lucky. Bernard looked down just as the poacher was being swept over the edge of the waterfall. Bernard didn't feel sorry for him — not one bit! It was hard to feel sorry for someone so cruel.

Marahute stopped to pick up Jake and Bianca. Then they were all on their way to take Cody home. As they flew past Marahute's nest, Wilbur let out a great sigh. "I hope that eagle hurries back," he said to himself. "If these eggs hatch before she returns, the chicks will think I'm their mother!"

As the mice and Cody soared on the back of the wonderful eagle, Bernard finally found the courage to ask Bianca to marry him.

"You are my hero!" sighed Bianca, as she gave Bernard a big kiss. "Of course I'll marry you. I thought you'd never ask!"

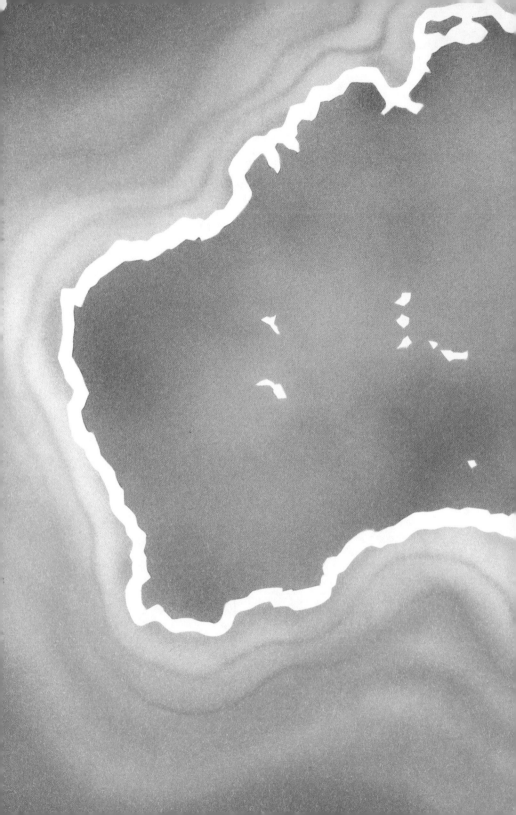